HERE'S **HEATHCLIFF** by Geo Gately

AMERICA'S CRAZIEST CAT!

Volume II

© McNaught Synd., Inc.

THE BEST OF SUNDAY WITH HEATHCLIFF

ONE, TWO, THREE, AND YOU'RE OUT

TOR

A TOM DOHERTY ASSOCIATES BOOK

HEATHCLIFF: ONE, TWO, THREE AND YOU'RE OUT
Volume II of HERE'S HEATHCLIFF

Copyright © 1981 by McNaught Syndicate, Inc.

Reprinted by arrangement with Windmill Books, Inc. and Simon and Schuster, a division of Gulf and Western Corp.

First Tor printing: January 1986

A TOR Book

Published by Tom Doherty Associates, Inc.
49 West 24 Street
New York, N.Y. 10010

ISBN: 0-812-56814-1
CAN. ED.: 0-812-56815-X

Printed in the United States of America

0 9 8 7 6 5 4 3 2

THE BREAKOUT

by Geo Gately

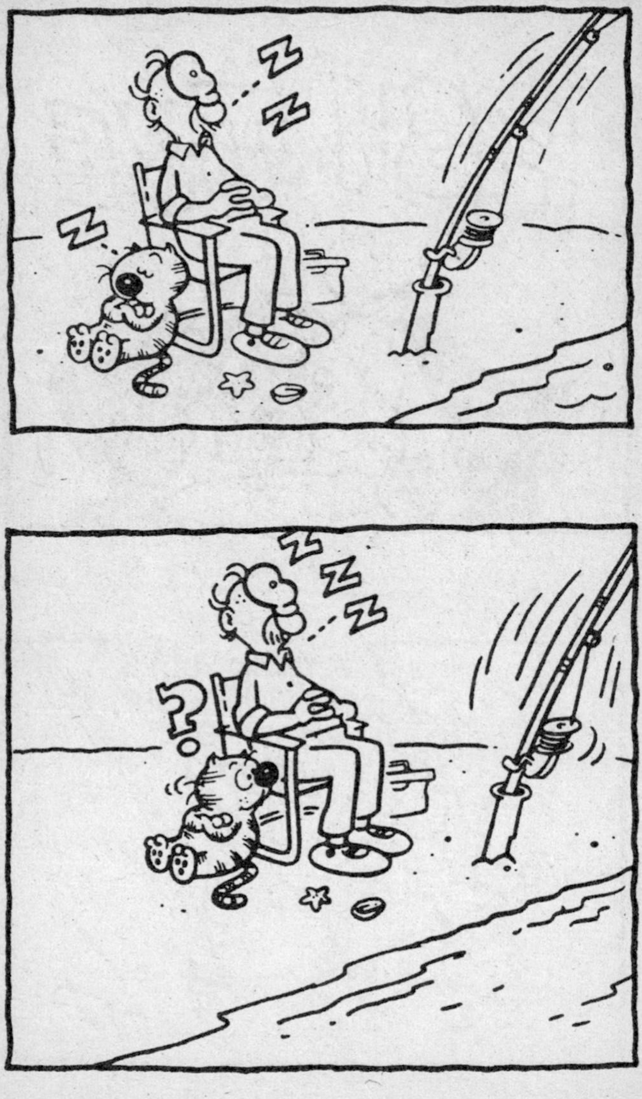

Z
Z
Z
Z
Z
Z
?

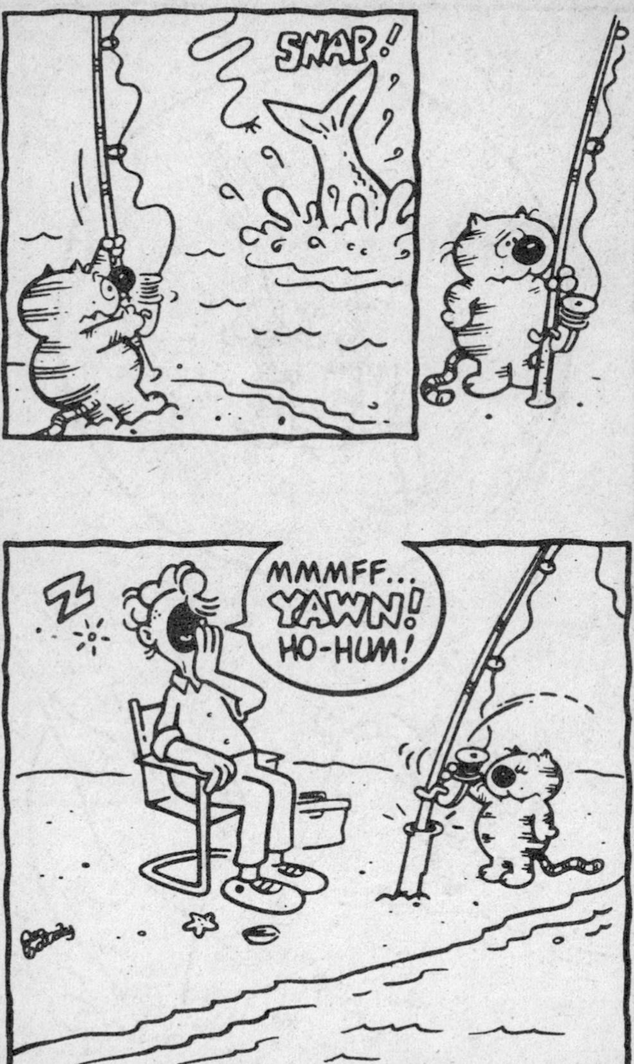
SNAP!
Z
MMMFF... YAWN! HO-HUM!

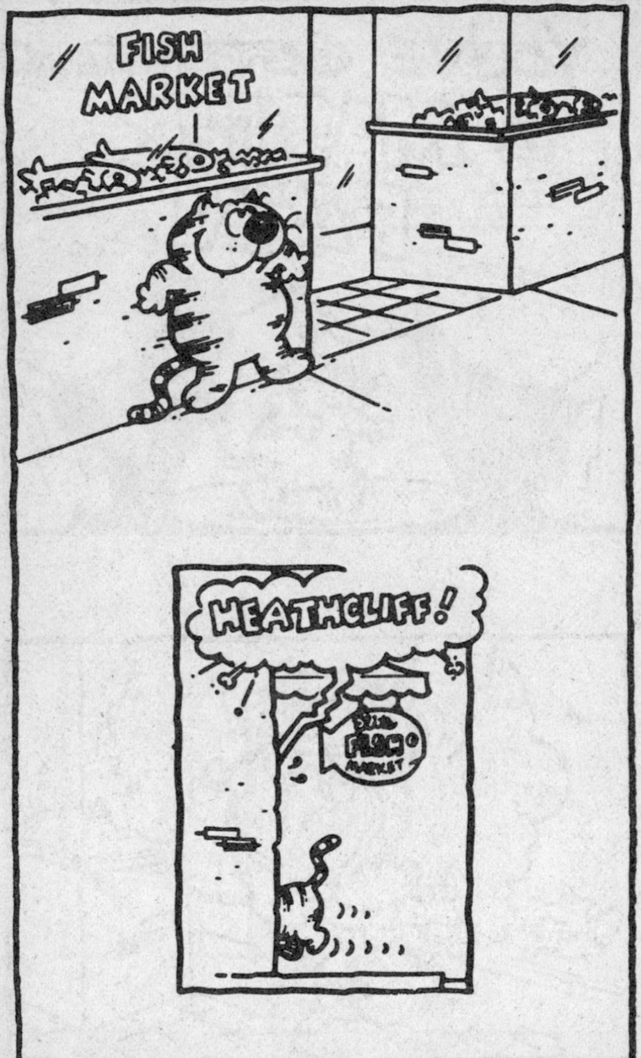
FISH MARKET
HEATHCLIFF!

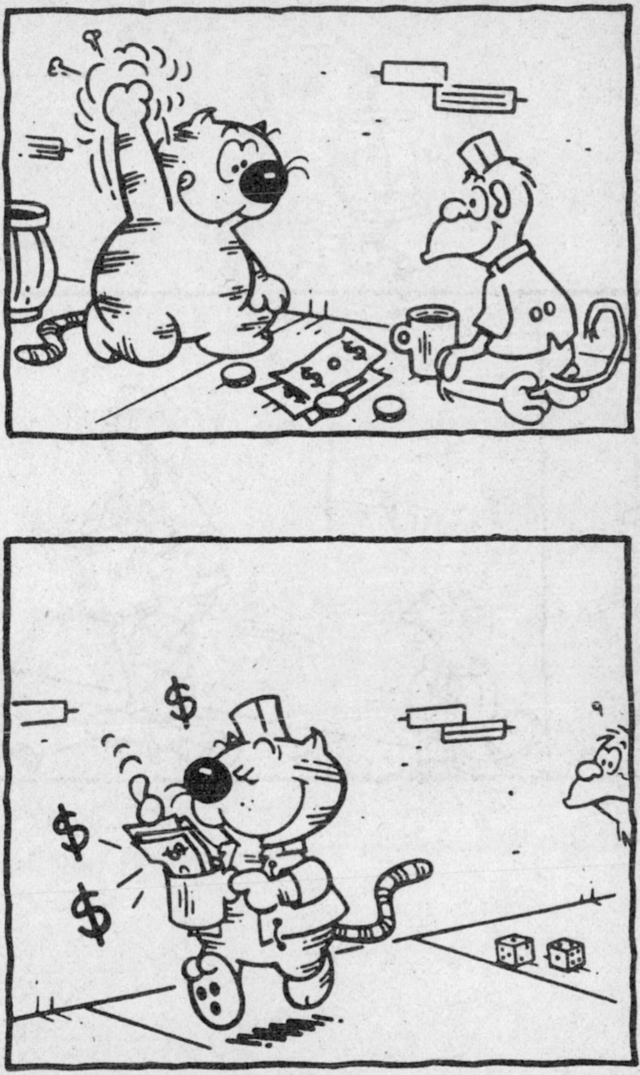

10-17 © 1976 McNaught Synd., Inc.

CITY
PARK

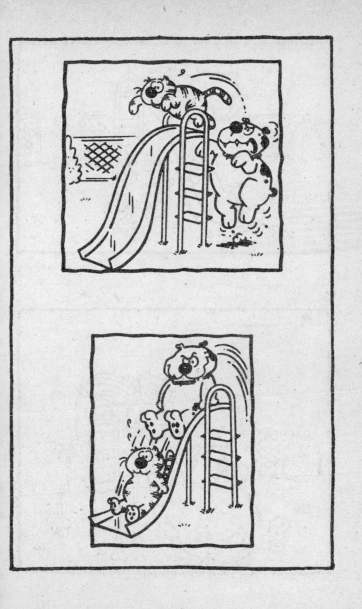

11-7 1976 McNaught Synd., Inc.

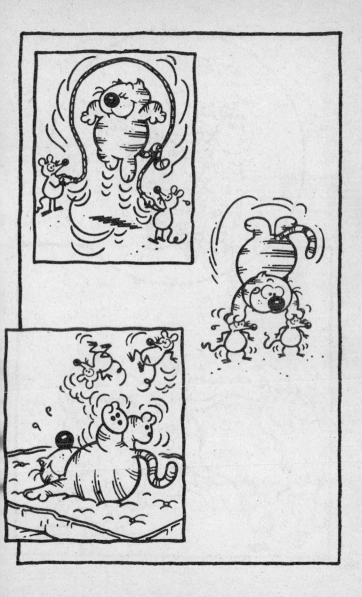

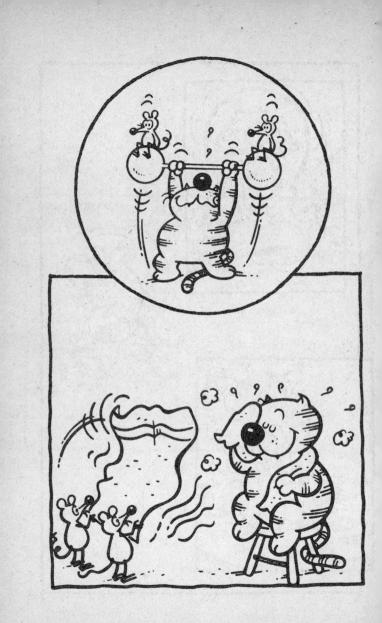

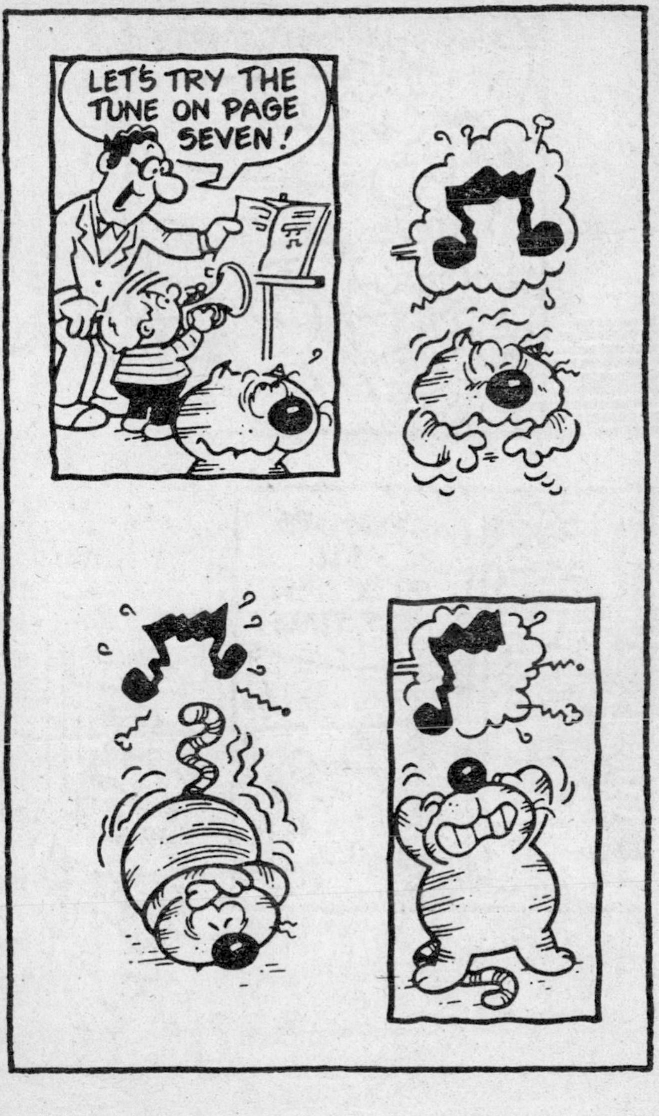
LET'S TRY THE TUNE ON PAGE SEVEN!

HOLIDAY REPRIEVE

by Geo Gately

12-26   1976
McNaught Synd., Inc.

HEATHCLIFF

AMERICA'S CRAZIEST CAT

☐ 56800-1   SPECIALTIES ON THE HOUSE $1.95
    56801-X   Canada $2.50

☐ 56802-8   HEATHCLIFF AT HOME $1.95
    56803-6   Canada $2.50

☐ 56804-4   HEATHCLIFF AND THE $1.95
    56805-2   GOOD LIFE   Canada $2.50

☐ 56806-0   HEATHCLIFF: ONE, TWO, THREE $1.95
    56807-9   AND YOU'RE OUT   Canada $2.50

Buy them at your local bookstore or use this handy coupon:
Clip and mail this page with your order

TOR BOOKS—Reader Service Dept.
49 W. 24 Street, 9th Floor, New York, NY 10010

Please send me the book(s) I have checked above. I am
enclosing $_____ (please add $1.00 to cover postage
and handling). Send check or money order only—
no cash or C.O.D.'s.

Mr./Mrs./Miss _____

Address _____

City _____ State/Zip _____
Please allow six weeks for delivery. Prices subject to
change without notice.